THE Riddle Monster

BY LISL WEIL

CLARION BOOKS

TICKNOR & FIELDS: A HOUGHTON MIFFLIN COMPANY

NEW YORK

Clarion Books, 52 Vanderbilt Avenue, New York, NY 10017
Copyright © 1980 by Lisl Weil   First Clarion Books Edition 1981
All rights reserved. This edition is published by CLARION BOOKS,
Ticknor & Fields, A Houghton Mifflin Company, by arrangement
with Scholastic Book Services, a division of Scholastic Magazines, Inc.
Printed in the United States of America.   1686

Library of Congress Cataloging in Publication Data
Weil, Lisl.   The riddle monster.   "Clarion books."
Summary: A horrible monster who eats anyone unable to answer
its riddle is given its just reward by a thoughtful prince.
[1. Monsters—Fiction. 2. Riddles—Fiction] I. Title.
PZ7.W433Ri   [E]   81-1030
ISBN 0-395-31019-9   AACR2

A LONG TIME AGO
there lived a monster who was
called the Sphinx. It had the head
of a woman, the body of a dog,
the wings of a bird, and the tail
of a serpent.

No doubt about it,
the monster was really terrible.
And ... it was *very* clever!

Its favorite hobby was thinking up riddles.
In fact, the monster had thought up
a riddle it was sure no one could solve.

Its second favorite hobby
was eating.
Especially eating people.
Yes, people!

Now, at that time, there were
very few roads for people to
take when they wanted to travel.

The monster
watched the roads
from its home
on a mountain top.

Whenever it was hungry,
which was rather often,
it would pick out one of the
travelers and fly down
to block the road.

Then it would shout out the riddle.

And when the traveler could not solve it . . .

SHHHGLUCK! The monster ate him up.

The monster grew fatter and FATTER and FATTER because no one could answer the riddle.

And people grew more and more frightened . . .

and tried to stay at home.

One day a prince came
riding down the road.
The prince was very good
at riddles, but the monster
did not know it.

"Aha," thought the monster.
"Here comes a tasty snack."
And it flew down from the mountain
and blocked the road.

"YOU CANNOT PASS," it shouted,
"UNLESS YOU CAN SOLVE MY RIDDLE."

"WHAT MOVES ON FOUR LEGS IN THE MORNING?
ON TWO LEGS AT NOON? AND ON THREE LEGS
IN THE EVENING?"

"That is a very hard riddle,"
  said the prince.
"YES," shouted the monster.
"AND YOU WILL NEVER GET IT."
"I know it is not a bird," said the prince.
"And surely it's not a fish. And it could
  not be any wild animal either."
"GIVE UP!" yelled the monster.
"I'M GETTING HUNGRY."
"No," said the prince. "I think
  I have the answer.
  It must be—is it—Man?"

"A baby crawls around on all fours.
That is morning—the morning of life.

A young man walks on two legs.
That is noon—the noon of life.

An old man walks on three legs
when he uses a cane.
That is evening—the evening of life."

The monster was furious.
"YOU GUESSED! YOU GUESSED!" it shouted.

It grew madder and madder, and
it puffed out in all directions,
until at last…

...It blew up!

From that day on, people were
no longer afraid to travel.
And everyone was grateful to the prince.

About the Author

Lisl Weil was born and educated in Vienna, Austria and now lives in New York City.

Every season for more than twenty years, Ms. Weil has appeared at Lincoln Center with the Little Orchestra Society's Young People's Concert, where she illustrates the story behind the music played by the orchestra. These performances have resulted in dramatic renderings of such favorite musical pieces as *Cinderella* and *A Midsummer Night's Dream*. She has also performed with many major symphony orchestras around the country as well as on national television.

Lisl Weil has written and illustrated many popular books for children. *The Riddle Monster* is her first for Clarion.

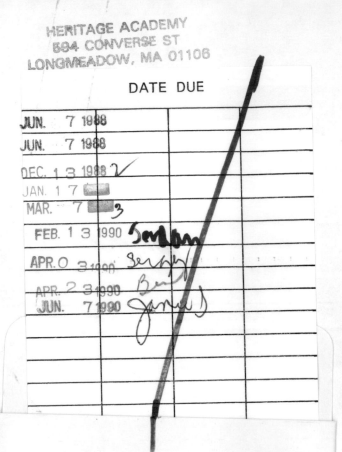

DATE DUE

JUN. 7 1988		
JUN. 7 1988		
DEC. 1 3 1988		
JAN. 1 7		
MAR. 7		
FEB. 1 3 1990		
APR. 0 3 1990		
APR. 2 3 1990		
JUN. 7 1990		

1 686

Weil, Lisl

   The riddle monster